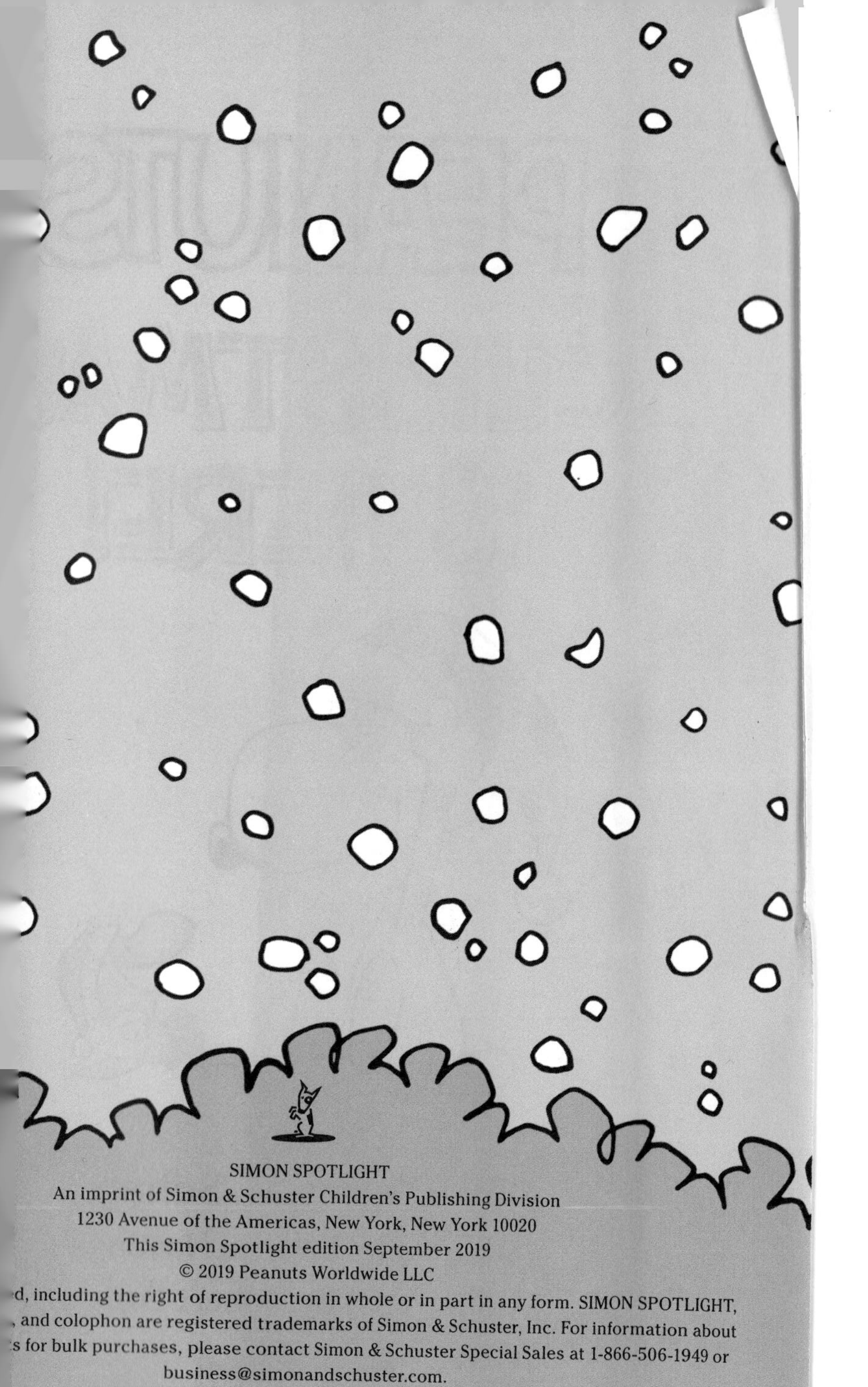

SIMON SPOTLIGHT
An imprint of Simon & Schuster Children's Publishing Division
1230 Avenue of the Americas, New York, New York 10020
This Simon Spotlight edition September 2019

Manufactured in the United States of America 0819 LAK
2 4 6 8 10 9 7 5 3 1
ISBN 978-1-5344-5056-1 (hc)
ISBN 978-1-5344-5055-4 (pbk)
ISBN 978-1-5344-5057-8 (eBook)

by Charles M

adapted by Ximen

illustrated by Ro

Ready-to-Re

Simon Spotli
New York London Toronto

Snoopy is sleeping on his
doghouse when something
wet hits his nose.

He opens his eyes and sees
snowflakes in the air!
Woodstock! he calls.

Look! It is finally snowing!
Christmas is coming!
Snoopy exclaims.

What do you want for Christmas this year? Snoopy asks Woodstock.
Woodstock chirps excitedly.
Well, yes, treats do make the best gifts, Snoopy replies.

This year I just want to have fun with my best friend, Snoopy says.
Woodstock agrees.
They spend the rest of the day planning holiday activities.

On Christmas Eve, Snoopy
and Woodstock are ready for fun!
First, they build a snowman.
They top it off with a Santa hat.

They are admiring their snowman
when Sally walks by.
“Good grief!” she shouts.
“That poor snowman needs eyes!
It needs a nose! *And* it is crooked!”

Woodstock chirps sadly.
Yes, I like it better our way too.
We were just having fun,
Snoopy says.

They leave Sally, who is too busy making changes to their snowman to notice.

Snoopy and Woodstock make their way to the top of a hill.
They are going sledding.
Yippee! This hill has the best snowflakes! Snoopy says.

"Excuse me!" Lucy suddenly yells.
Where did she come from?
Snoopy wonders.
"I am queen of this hill!
If you want to be here, you must
meet all of my demands!" Lucy says.

Lucy pulls out a long list.
“First, you must always call me Queen Lucy. Second, you must hunt Christmas treasures for me. Third . . .”
Snoopy and Woodstock decide not to hear the third demand. They grab the sled and walk away.

Snoopy and Woodstock hop
on the sled.
They glide gracefully down the hill.

Snoopy and Woodstock land
on a frozen lake.
*This is perfect! Now let's
go ice-skating!* Snoopy cheers.

Woodstock cheers him on. Snoopy focuses and gathers up speed . . . when suddenly Franklin and Schroeder come racing toward him!

Snoopy practices his moves on
the ice.
He twirls, he jumps, and . . .
he lands on his bottom!
Snoopy needs a *lot* more practice.

"Watch out!" calls Franklin, a little too late.
"Want to join our hockey game?" asks Schroeder.
Snoopy declines the invitation as Woodstock tries to help him up.

Snoopy is frustrated.
All I wanted was to make this a fun Christmas for Woodstock, but everything is going wrong,
Snoopy thinks.

I know just the thing to get us into the holiday spirit,
Snoopy suddenly says.
Singing Christmas carols!
They put on Santa hats
and head into town.

Snoopy grabs a microphone
and sings.
Woodstock grabs a bell and rings.
They are the perfect pair!

Just then Charlie Brown and Linus appear.
Charlie Brown is confused.
"I always thought Santa Claus said, '*ho, ho, ho,*' not '*woof, woof, woof,*'" he comments.

Snoopy sighs.
He and Woodstock decide to go home, but Snoopy has not given up on the fun just yet.
Let's decorate my doghouse, he suggests.

Snoopy and Woodstock collect every ornament they can find and decorate the doghouse.
Then they bake some treats.

Snoopy and Woodstock are tired.
They take a snack break.
Suddenly Snoopy realizes
something.

No one is interrupting them.
Nobody is spoiling their fun.
And yet, it feels *too* quiet.

Where is everyone? Snoopy asks.
Woodstock chirps.
You are right, Snoopy admits.
Christmas Eve has been fun,
but it is not the same without
everyone being together.

I was so focused on our own fun that I forgot about everyone else's fun. No one will want to spend Christmas with me ever again! Snoopy says.

Woodstock has an idea that he
hopes will cheer Snoopy up.
He quickly flies away.

Even my best friend is leaving me on Christmas Eve, Snoopy thinks. Just then Snoopy hears voices nearby.

Suddenly Woodstock arrives with the whole gang!
Now Christmas is here!
Snoopy exclaims.
Merry Christmas!